Sam went to the book sale.

1

He wanted a book about spiders.

He looked at a book about a baby.

He wanted to give it to Jack.

Sam gave the books to Mrs Hall.
Then he gave his money to Mrs Hall.

7

Mrs Hall looked at his money.

She said, 'Sorry, Sam.
You haven't got enough money.'

Sam looked at the books.

He put the baby book back.

He took the book about spiders.

Floating and Flying

Then he got some paper
and some pens.

14

Sam made a book
about a baby and . . .

he gave it to Jack.